The Boy Behind My Face

Written by: **James Mcleod Jr** with **Jenifer C. Orefice**

Illustrated by: **Taylor Coleman**

Smile and let your happy Shine

James McLeod :)

My name is James.

And I am a **SUPERHERO.**

I don't have any special, magical powers.

But I scared a monster away.

The monster didn't hide under
my bed, like the usual kind.

He didn't tiptoe around my
room at night in the shadows.

Nope, not this monster.

This monster was with me every day.

As soon as I woke up in the morning and looked in the mirror, he was there!

I would duck and try not to look, but I knew he was there.

Other people saw him too. They pointed,
they stared, and said mean things.

It made me sad. And scared.

And I didn't know what to do about it, because the scary monster in the mirror was me!!

I was born looking different than everyone else. I am different colors.

I don't look like everyone else, and I just want to be the same! I don't want people to stare and point and ooh and aah! I don't want to be a monster!

But I didn't know what to do about it!

And then, one day, I came home from school crying and fell asleep with my head under the pillow.

And when I woke up, everything changed!

I didn't want to cry anymore! I didn't want
to be sad! I didn't want to be lonely!

And I knew what I had to do!

I stood up straight and marched
myself to the bathroom mirror.

At first, I saw the monster again!
And I almost ducked away!

But I knew I couldn't do that anymore.

I had to be **BRAVE.**

I had to be **STRONG.**

I looked and I looked and I looked in the mirror, until, slowly, the monster started fading further and further away.

I noticed my kind eyes for the first time!

My beautiful, amazing smile!

I was beautiful! I was shining beauty from the inside out!

I didn't look like anyone else in the whole world, and I loved it! It was amazing!

I had chased the monster away!!!!

No magic power, no magic spell. I did it just by being brave!

The next day at school, the kids started to tease. But I didn't cry, I smiled at them!

The day after that, the kids didn't tease.

The day after that, one of the kids sat next to me at lunch.

And day after day got a little bit better.

I chased the monster away!

And maybe I am a superhero after all!

Maybe my superpowers are

BRAVERY, KINDNESS, and LOVE!